STEP RIGHT UP! STEP RIGHT UP!

The carnival is in town! And it's raising funds for Bear Country Hospital. But something's not quite right. Even Ralph Ripoff, the town scam artist, wonders just what kind of funny business is going on in the funhouse trailer...

BIG CHAPTER BOOKS

The Berenstain Bears
IN THE
FREAKY FUNHOUSE

by the Berenstains

A BIG CHAPTER BOOK™

Random House New York

Library of Congress Cataloging-in-Publication Data
Berenstain, Stan.
The Berenstain bears in the freaky funhouse /
by Stan and Jan Berenstain.
  p. cm. — (A big chapter book)
SUMMARY: Brother and Sister Bear and several other cubs become suspicious when Ralph Ripoff becomes involved in efforts to raise money to build a new wing for the local hospital.
ISBN 0-679-87244-2 (pbk.) — ISBN 0-679-97244-7 (lib. bdg.)
[1. Swindlers and swindling—Fiction. 2. Bears—Fiction.
I. Berenstain, Jan. II. Title.
III. Series: Berenstain, Stan. Big chapter book.
PZ7.B4483Berk 1995
[Fic]—dc20 94-47956

Contents

Chapter 1
A Gruesome Twosome?

Most of the Bear Country cubs loved summer more than any other season. Summer meant fun. It meant warm weather, games, summer camp—and, best of all, *no school*.

Not that school was all bad. It could be very interesting. But it could also be boring. And when it was boring, all you could do was wait for it to get interesting again.

It was different being bored in the summer, especially before summer camp started. Instead of sitting in the school cafeteria at lunch staring at your shepherd's pie, you could get together with your friends for burgers and shakes at the Burger Bear. You could even plan something fun for after lunch.

And that's exactly what Brother and Sister Bear, Cousin Fred, and Queenie McBear did one bright summer day. They sat in their favorite booth at the Burger Bear and traded ideas.

Brother wanted to get teams together for a softball game. Sister wanted to fly kites. Queenie was so set on spending the afternoon playing video games at the mall that Brother and Sister finally agreed on that. But Fred was against all video games.

"They just rot your brain," he said. "Even softball is better for the mind."

"Oh, yeah?" said Queenie. "How?"

"The machine keeps score for you in a video game," said Fred. "In softball, at least, you have to keep count of balls and strikes all by yourself."

"Oh, gimme a break!" moaned Queenie. She turned away from Fred in disgust and looked out the window. "Hey, look," she said, pointing across the street at the front entrance of Bear Country Hospital. "Isn't that Mama and Papa Bear coming out of the hospital? What's wrong, Brother? Is

Grizzly Gramps or Gran sick?"

"No, they're fine," said Brother. "Mama and Papa are on the hospital building-fund committee. They just had a meeting."

Brother explained that Dr. Gert Grizzly, president of the hospital, was trying to raise money to build a new wing for the hospital. He pointed to a sign on the hospital lawn. It showed a big thermometer with the red mercury inside shooting up through a dollar sign.

"Nice sign," said Cousin Fred. "Clever, isn't it, Queenie?"

But Queenie wasn't looking at the sign. She had her eye on the hospital entrance. "Hey, there's Dr. Gert," she said. "And look who she's with!"

"Ralph Ripoff!" said Sister with a gasp. Ralph was the town's biggest small-time crook.

The cubs just stared for a moment. There was Dr. Gert Grizzly, one of Bear Country's most honest and respected citizens, talking with the famous swindler. It was indeed a strange sight. And they weren't just talking. Ralph was all smiles and chuckles, and Gert was smiling back. She was even giggling.

"Do you think they're a twosome?" Fred asked Queenie.

"A *gruesome* twosome, if you ask me," said Queenie.

"Maybe Ralph has eyes for Dr. Gert," said Sister.

Brother shook his head. "The only thing Ralph has eyes for, Sis, is other bears' money."

"But Dr. Gert is hanging on Ralph's every word," said Queenie. "That kind of worries me."

"Dr. Gert is a real smart cookie," said Fred. "She's not going to fall for any of Ralph's schemes."

"Probably not," agreed Queenie. "But maybe she's falling for *Ralph*."

The cubs watched as Ralph and Dr. Gert walked slowly down the street, chatting as they went. They stopped at a popular restaurant. Ralph opened the front door for Dr. Gert and followed her inside.

"Looks like they're having lunch at The

Red Lantern," said Brother. "Let's go take a peek."

The cubs paid for their lunches and hurried down the street to The Red Lantern. White curtains hung from a thick brass curtain rod along the lower part of the restaurant's wide front window. The cubs got on their tiptoes to peek over the curtains.

"There they are," said Queenie. "At the back, over in the corner."

Ralph and Dr. Gert had settled into a cozy booth. They were still chatting happily.

"What do you think's going on?" asked Sister.

"Beats me," said Brother. "And I don't think we're going to find out as long as they're in there. Unless, that is, one of you can hear through windows."

Deep in thought, the cubs headed back down the street. No one said a word until they passed the big sign on the hospital lawn.

"Stop!" cried Queenie all of a sudden. She pointed at the sign. *"Raising money,"* she said. *"Ralph Ripoff* and *raising money* …anyone see a connection?"

The cubs were silent.

"Come on, guys," said Queenie. "Use your heads! Why do you think Ralph would be so charming to someone who is trying to raise a lot of money?"

"Hmm," said Cousin Fred. "I see what you mean." He thought for a moment, then shook his head. "But not even *Ralph* could

expect to get his hands on the money Dr. Gert's raising for the new hospital wing."

"I sure hope you're right," said Queenie.

"So, what're we doing this afternoon?" asked Fred.

"I don't know," said Queenie. "You really shot down my video game idea, that's for sure. But I thought it over, and it does make sense, what you said about them rotting our brains. Too bad, though. I hear there's a

ANYONE SEE A CONNECTION?

brand-new Stargazer game at the mall. They say it's great for astronomy buffs..." Queenie winked at Brother and Sister.

Fred looked off into the sky as if he were gazing at distant stars. "Well," he said, "maybe for a few minutes..."

"Great!" said Queenie. "Let's go!"

As the cubs took off for the mall, Ralph Ripoff and Dr. Gert Grizzly were sharing a king-size baked salmon at The Red Lantern.

"Now that you mention it, dear," Ralph was saying, "I've had some experience in separating folks from their mon—er, raising funds. I just might have some ideas about how to raise money for your new hospital wing."

"That's wonderful, Ralph!" said Gert. "Please, tell me!"

Chapter 2
Putty in Their Hands

Later that afternoon, Ralph Ripoff strolled along the forest path to his houseboat. He was twirling his walking stick and looking very pleased with himself. "Yes, sir," he muttered. "Putty in my hands!"

The forest gloom gave way to bright sunlight when Ralph reached the river. As he walked up the gangplank of his houseboat, he could hear his pet parrot inside screeching, "Ringing off the hook! Ringing off the hook!"

Ralph stepped inside. Sure enough, the phone was ringing.

"All right, cool it, you birdbrain!" he yelled at the parrot. He picked up the phone. "Well, Captain Billy! How's my old circus buddy today? Yes, indeed. Everything's under control. The good doctor is like putty in my hands. Will she sign? Of course, she'll sign. But don't forget our deal. I control all the games on the midway..."

Some miles away, on the main highway into Beartown, Captain Billy hung up the car phone in the cab of his truck. He was leading a long line of other trucks. On the side of the cab, the words CAPTAIN BILLY'S COLOSSAL CIRCUS AND CARNIVAL were printed in large fancy letters. And below that: *Fundraising a Specialty*.

Captain Billy turned to the driver, a big, tough-looking fellow named Otto, and said,

"Ralph says the hospital deal is all set. Says this Gert Grizzly is putty in his hands."

"Can we trust him?" asked Otto. His voice sounded like truck tires on gravel.

Billy smiled and looked off into the distance. "Ralph and I used to work carnivals together in the old days—picking pockets, running midway games…"

"But can we trust him?"

"About as far as I can throw him," said Billy. He had stopped smiling.

"Well, if he messes up," growled Otto, "*he'll* be putty in *my* hands."

Otto raised a huge hand from the steering wheel, squeezed it into a fist, and then squeezed it some more. His knuckles cracking sounded like a string of firecrackers.

That made Billy smile again. Otto was just about the strongest bear he had ever seen. On the side of one of the circus trucks rumbling along behind them was a painting of Primo the World's Strongest Bear. In the painting, Primo looked a lot like Otto.

In fact, he looked *exactly* like Otto.

Chapter 3
Cub Gossip

That evening, at the Bear family tree house, the Bears were having dinner. After seeing the "gruesome twosome," Brother and Sister couldn't wait to hear all about the hospital fundraising meeting.

"How'd your meeting go, Papa?" asked Brother.

"Meeting?" said Papa.

"At the hospital," said Brother. "We were across the street at the Burger Bear. We saw you come out."

"Oh, *that* meeting. It went fine."

"That's not all we saw," said Sister. "We

DR. GERT AND RALPH?
NO KIDDING?

saw Dr. Gert Grizzly and Ralph Ripoff together. And they were a *twosome!*"

"Dr. Gert and *Ralph?*" said Papa. "No kidding?"

"That will be quite enough, cubs," said Mama. "I won't stand for any cub gossip about grownups."

Sister said, "Queenie thinks it has something to do with—"

"Please spare me any wisdom from Queenie," said Mama. "Now, finish your dinner."

Later, Mama and Papa were in the kitchen alone doing the dishes. The cubs had gone out to play in the yard for the last hour or two of daylight.

"Gert and *Ralph!*" said Papa, shaking his head. "Wow!"

"What do you suppose is going on?" asked Mama.

Papa shrugged. "Beats me."

"Do you suppose what Sister said is true? About Ralph and Gert being a twosome?"

"But you just said you didn't believe any cub gossip!" said Papa.

"I said I wouldn't *stand* for any cub gossip," said Mama. "Not that I didn't believe it."

"Hmm," said Papa. He scrubbed the inside of a pot as he thought. Suddenly he frowned. "Naw! That's impossible. What could Gert ever see in Ralph?"

"Well, he *can* be quite charming," said Mama.

"What d'ya mean 'charming'?" said Papa. "Don't you think *I'm* charming?"

"Of course I do—"

"Then why'd you say *Ralph's* charming?"

Mama just sighed. "Never mind, dear," she said. "Forget I ever brought it up."

NEVER MIND, DEAR...

Chapter 4
Circus!

The next morning, Sister still wanted to fly kites and Brother still wanted to play softball. They argued about it at breakfast. Little did they know that something had just happened that would take care of all their plans for several days to come.

They were cleaning up their breakfast dishes when they heard a voice outside shouting, "Brother! Sister! Come quick!" Brother ran to the front door and opened it. There were Queenie and Cousin Fred, standing at the foot of the steps.

"What's all the excitement about?" asked Brother.

"The circus! The circus!" cried Fred. "It just came to town!"

"Come on!" said Queenie. "Let's watch 'em set up!"

The cubs told Mama where they were going and joined their friends. They ran all the way out to the main highway and, within minutes, stood before the big empty patch of ground by the freight yard.

But the big empty patch of ground wasn't
empty anymore. It was filled with trucks,
rides, and game booths. Workers were busy
setting up the circus.

Wide-eyed, the cubs explored the
grounds.

"Wow, look at that guy!" said Sister. She
pointed at the picture of Primo the World's
Strongest Bear.

"Pretty cool," said Brother. "But look over there!"

Brother had spied the circus's lead truck. But it wasn't the cab with the *Captain Billy's* sign that he was staring at. It was the long trailer in back.

On both sides of it was the coolest painting the cubs had ever seen.

There were spider webs in the corners and evil-eyed bats hanging upside down all along the top. At the bottom, a row of strange little creatures with pointy ears and huge bloodshot eyes peered out from the gloom. Along the middle, glowing against the purplish black background, loomed terrifying witches, goblins, and demons. And at the back, in between two openings with curtains over them, stood the huge Frankenbear Monster.

Spooky red letters on either side of the trailer and above the Monster said FREAKY FUNHOUSE. Smaller letters beneath the Monster said WARNING: *Only bears with strong hearts may enter!*

Slowly, the cubs walked around the trailer, staring. Queenie stopped to read the warning out loud. She turned to Sister and chuckled. "Do you have a strong heart, Sis?"

Sister said nothing. She had put her hands over her eyes and was looking up at the Frankenbear Monster through the cracks between her fingers.

Brother winked at Queenie and Fred. "Her heart must be strong," he said, "because I can hear it way over here. And it's goin' a mile a minute."

"Quit it!" said Sister.

"I think you'd better skip the Freaky Funhouse and go on that ride instead," said Queenie, pointing to a ride for young cubs. A worker was testing it. Giant teacups on giant saucers glided in slow circles.

"I don't know, Queenie," said Brother with another wink. "Looks dangerous. Sis could get hit with a giant cube of sugar…"

Sister jerked her hands away from her eyes and balled them up into fists. "Cut it out!" she cried. "You wanna see *dangerous?* Just keep talkin'—!"

Suddenly the door of the cab opened. The cubs gasped. Was it a witch? A demon? The Frankenbear Monster?!

No, it was just a bear wearing a sea captain's hat. He climbed down from the cab and jabbed a thumb at the sign. "I run the show around here," he said.

"Then you must be Captain Billy," said Sister.

"Good guess," said the bear. "How'd you find out we were in town?"

"A cub named Too-Tall told us," said Queenie.

"Oh, that one," said Captain Billy with a frown. "Him and his band of wild animals were here about an hour ago. I kicked 'em out, told 'em not to come back until we open tonight."

"Why?" asked Sister.

"They were playin' some kind of leapfrog

game in and out of those teacups over there," said Billy. "Busted the whole dang ride. We just now got it workin' again."

Billy looked off toward town. "Soon as word gets around, we'll be downright swamped with sightseers," he said. "Hey, here come some now."

But there were no sightseers in Police Chief Bruno's car. Just Chief Bruno and Officer Marguerite. They drove right up to the Freaky Funhouse and got out. Captain Billy introduced himself.

"Bet you know why we're here, Captain Billy," said Chief Bruno.

"Now, let me guess," said Billy. He took a piece of paper from his shirt pocket, unfolded it, and handed it to the chief. "Signed by Mayor Horace J. Honeypot himself, Chief."

"So it is," said Chief Bruno. "Nothing wrong with this permit. You clearly have the right to bring your circus to Beartown."

The chief looked around the grounds. He seemed suspicious. "But what about the safety of these rides?" he asked.

"Safest rides in the business," said Billy. He pointed to a license attached to the Freaky Funhouse. "You'll find one of these on each and every ride and attraction, Chief. Why, I'd let my own cubs ride 'em a thousand times. If I had any cubs, that is."

Chief Bruno went to look at a few of the

rides and came back. "Everything checks out," he said. But he looked around again as if something were bothering him.

Just then another car drove up.

"Say, isn't that Gert Grizzly's car?" said Officer Marguerite.

Ralph Ripoff hopped out of the passenger's side and hurried over to open the driver's door for Dr. Gert. She got out and put her arm in Ralph's.

"Oh, dear," she said when she noticed Chief Bruno. "I hope you haven't found any problems with my friend's circus, Chief. Captain Billy has generously agreed to raise funds for the new hospital wing."

The chief took off his cap and scratched his head. "Well, I'll be darned," he said. "So *that's* why the circus is in town."

"Yes," said Dr. Gert. "A large share of the money taken in by the circus will go

to the hospital building fund."

"That's right, Chief," said Ralph with a big grin. "As a matter of fact, the good doctor is here to sign the contract right now."

Ralph reached for Dr. Gert's arm, but Chief Bruno beat him to it. The chief led her a few yards away. He was frowning. In a low voice, he said, "Now, you look over that contract very carefully before signing it, Gert."

"Don't worry, Chief," she said. "I never sign anything without reading it first."

"And make sure you get a copy of it."

"Of course, Chief."

Dr. Gert went back to Ralph's side. "After you, my dear," he said, and helped her up into the truck office, which was between the cab and the Freaky Funhouse.

"Well," said Chief Bruno to Captain Billy. "Everything seems to be in order. I hope you make a lot of money." He looked hard at Captain Billy. "For the new hospital wing, I mean."

The chief and Officer Marguerite got in their car and drove away.

Captain Billy was about to join Ralph and Dr. Gert in the office when he stopped and turned back to the cubs. "It's always been my practice," he said, "to hire a few bright local cubs to give out circus posters, run errands, and help around the circus. Think you can handle it?"

The cubs nodded so fast and hard they

looked like wind-up toys gone haywire.

Captain Billy climbed into the office and came back with a stack of posters. "Here you go," he said. "And here's your pay for helping out. Free passes to all rides and attractions, signed by Captain Billy himself. Now, off you go."

In their excitement, the cubs forgot all about the worried look they'd noticed on Chief Bruno's face. Off to town they ran, as fast as their legs could carry them.

Chapter 5
Swindler Meets Sucker

Captain Billy's office looked like a mini-circus. A skeleton stood in one corner, a gorilla suit in another. A coiled bullwhip hung on one wall, and a life-size painting of Coco the Clown hung on the opposite wall.

Dr. Gert stood in the middle of the room

and looked around. It was so exciting! She felt almost as if she were joining the circus!

"Now, you sit right over there, dear," said Captain Billy. "Here's the contract. Just sign on the dotted line, and Captain Billy's Colossal Circus and Carnival will start making money for your wonderful new hospital wing."

"But not without reading it first, my dear," said Ralph.

Dr. Gert took out her reading glasses and put them on. " 'Eighty percent of all money will go to the hospital and twenty percent to the circus,' " she read. "Why, that's very generous, Captain."

"We normally go fifty-fifty," said Billy. "But your cause is such a good one, and Ralph here is such a dear friend…"

"He *is* dear, isn't he?" said Dr. Gert. She took the pen that Ralph held out to her and signed on the dotted line.

Billy placed more papers in front of Dr. Gert. "Here are three more copies of the contract for you to sign," he said. "One for you, one for our main office, and one for the mayor's office."

As Dr. Gert signed the copies of the contract, Captain Billy put his hand to his mouth to hide a smile. *He* knew they weren't really copies. Only on the very first contract—the one Dr. Gert had read before signing—did eighty percent of the money go to the hospital. On all the other "copies," eighty percent went to the *circus!* And not only that. All the expenses of running the circus—wages, electricity, water, insurance—came out of the hospital's twenty percent!

What a sucker! thought Captain Billy as he watched Dr. Gert sign the contracts. *She*

WHAT A SUCKER!

CONTRACT

Dr. GGringly

didn't read past that first phony copy! It works every time!

Billy showed Ralph and Dr. Gert out of the office. At that very moment, a cry went up nearby. A rope on the main tent had snapped, and the whole thing was about to collapse! Quick as a wink, Otto was there. He held it up by pure strength while a group of workers fixed it.

"My goodness!" said Dr. Gert. "Did you see what he did?"

Billy pointed to the poster of Primo the World's Strongest Bear. "Otto isn't just my main helper," he said. "We all do double duty here. I'm also the ringmaster."

"How exciting!" said Dr. Gert.

"See that fellow over there?" said Billy, pointing to a bear with a big, bushy beard. "He's Belinda the Bearded Lady."

"But—"

"Believe me, Gert, he's *gorgeous* in a low-cut evening gown."

Dr. Gert frowned. "But is that *honest?*" she said.

"My dear lady," said Billy. "This is *show business!* Speaking of 'honest,' why not let Ralph show you his own special circus kingdom. Mr. Midway, we used to call him. He's the crookedest—er, finest—games operator in the business. Well, if you'll excuse me, I have to go file my copy of the contract."

Meanwhile, the cubs had returned from their poster job. They followed Ralph and Dr. Gert down the midway, where game booths were set up on either side.

"Get away from me, cubs, ya bother me," muttered Ralph.

"You don't understand, Ralph," said Brother. "Captain Billy made us official circus helpers. We're free to go anywhere, anytime."

"In that case," said Ralph, "I might be

able to use you. Take a look at my ring-toss game here. The sucker—er, player—tries to win valuable prizes by tossing the rings over them."

As they strolled down the midway, Ralph pointed out other booths. "And here's the Walking Charlie," he said. "Four of the hats

are made of felt, and the fifth is wood painted to look like a tin can. Throw a baseball, knock off a felt hat, and win a prize. Or knock over the 'tin can' attached to the dummy's head and win a really big prize. And here's our milk-bottle game. To win, all you have to do is knock a stack of wooden milk bottles off a table."

The cubs were all smiles. They couldn't wait to try the games when the circus opened that evening.

But Dr. Gert seemed nervous. "Are you sure it's right to raise money with games of chance?" she asked Ralph.

"Oh, I think that would be absolutely, positively *wrong,* my dear," said Ralph. "But these are games of *skill.* Watch this."

Ralph switched on the Walking Charlie, grabbed a baseball, and knocked off one of the felt hats with a well-aimed throw. "Here," he said, handing a baseball to Brother. "You try it."

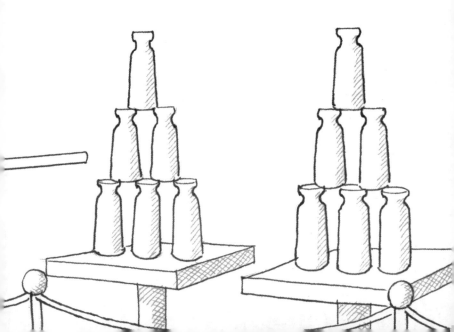

Brother took careful aim at the "tin can." He hit it right in the center, and over it went. But it popped right back up again.

The cubs finished touring the midway, taking special note of the prizes on display. Many of them were just cheap little dolls. But there were also radios and flashlights— even a boom box.

And pretty soon the cubs would each get a shot at those great prizes! They could hardly wait!

Chapter 6
Bucks, Moolah, and Long Green

That evening, bears from all over Bear Country crowded into Captain Billy's Colossal Circus and Carnival. There was so much to see and do!

In the big tent, there were clowns and jugglers, magicians and sword swallowers. Primo the World's Strongest Bear bent iron bars and broke chains across his huge chest. Belinda the Bearded Lady was indeed gorgeous in a low-cut evening gown.

Outside, Ralph Ripoff's piercing voice rose above the noise of the crowd: "Step right up! Step right up! Win valuable prizes!"

Since Ralph was busy working, Dr. Gert had come with Mama, Papa, and Farmer and Mrs. Ben. Papa and Farmer Ben felt like cubs again. They spent most of their time on the midway, throwing baseballs and tossing rings. But even though they spent a lot of money, they didn't win a single valuable prize—just a bunch of cheap little dolls.

It was the same for everyone on the midway. But no one seemed to care. After all, most of the money was going to a wonderful cause.

Brother, Sister, Fred, and Queenie made good use of their free passes. They went on every ride at least twice. As closing time approached, only one attraction was left. *The Freaky Funhouse.*

Trying to act cool about it, the cubs walked to the funhouse and stared up at the

huge spooky painting. Lit only by red, green, and purple neon lights, it was spookier than ever.

Sister looked up at the evil-eyed bats and creepy little creatures. Cousin Fred looked up at the witches, goblins, and demons. Queenie and Brother gazed at the Frankenbear Monster. And they all listened to the screams and howls coming from inside.

Suddenly their mouths went dry. Their knees shook and their hearts raced.

"You know," said Brother, "if we go in tonight, we won't have anything new to do tomorrow night."

"Yeah," said Queenie. "We've done everything else already."

"Let's leave it for tomorrow night," said Cousin Fred.

Sister opened her mouth to agree. But nothing came out. So she just nodded. Then the cubs split up to look for their parents.

Meanwhile, back at the midway, the Bears and Bens were asking Dr. Gert if she needed a ride home.

"No thanks, folks," said the doctor. "Ralph and I are planning a late supper."

"I hear you've been seeing a lot of Ralph lately," said Papa. "Ouch!" Mama had just elbowed him in the ribs.

"Why, yes," said Dr. Gert. "Yesterday we had a lovely picnic on the banks of Great Roaring River. We even went in for a swim!"

Ralph came strolling merrily back from the office, where he had just delivered a box full of money. "The take was tremendous, my dear!" he said to Dr. Gert.

"Take?" she said.

"The bucks," said Ralph. "The moolah. The long green. You know—*money*. There'll be plenty for a wing, my sweet. Why, there might even be enough for a drumstick!" He chuckled. "Well, ta-ta, friends."

Off into the night went Ralph, arm in arm with Dr. Gert.

Farmer Ben stared after them with a sour look on his face. "Humph," he said. "That swindler is no friend of mine. Wouldn't trust him as far as I can throw my prize bull."

"*He's* the one who can throw the bull," said Papa. "Did you hear all those 'my dears' and 'my sweets'?"

"I don't think that's fair," said Mama. "They seem quite fond of each other."

"You see, Mama?" said Sister. "I *told* you they're a twosome."

"And *I* told *you* that I don't want you discussing grownups' private business," scolded Mama.

"But, Mama," said Brother. "With all the fundraising for the hospital going on, Dr. Gert and Ralph dating isn't private business. It's *public* business."

"Hmm," said Farmer Ben after a brief silence. "The boy's got a point."

Later, when the cubs were lying in their bunk beds and ready for sleep, Brother made another good point.

"I've been thinking, Sis," he said. "Ralph did a whole lot of business on the midway tonight. But *no one* won a valuable prize. Just cheap little dolls."

Sister hugged the doll Papa had won for her. "I *love* my cheap little doll," she said sleepily.

"Think about it, Sis," said Brother. "Not one valuable prize!"

"So?"

"So tomorrow we're going out there early," said Brother.

"To do what?" asked Sister.

"A little detective work," said Brother.

Chapter 7
Crookeder Than
a Dog's Hind Leg

The four cub helpers got into the circus early the next day by showing their special passes. They headed straight for the midway. Workers were busy tightening tent ropes and oiling rides, and no one paid the cubs any attention.

"Ah, the circus!" said Cousin Fred. "When I was little, my favorite book was *Toby Bear of the Circus*. It was about a cub who runs off with the circus. I've always wondered what that would be like."

Sister shivered. It sounded much too scary for her.

Brother looked down the midway. "Okay," he said. "There's nobody here. Let's check out the games before Ralph shows up."

The cubs slipped into the ring-toss booth. The prizes sat on blocks of wood. To win, you had to hit the prize so that the ring slid down over both the prize and the block of wood.

Brother grabbed a ring and tested several prizes. The ring fit easily over the cheap dolls and their wooden blocks. But it fit *just barely* over the wooden blocks under the valuable prizes.

"This is a cheat!" said Brother. "It's almost impossible to win a valuable prize!"

They moved on to the milk-bottle game. Cousin Fred started lifting the bottles stacked on one of the tables. When he got to the bottom row of bottles, he let out a groan. "Wow!" he said. "They must be weighted down with lead! Nobody could knock these onto the floor. It's a complete ripoff!"

"Someone mention my name?" said a voice behind them.

The cubs turned to see Ralph Ripoff's smiling face just outside the booth.

"Ralph!" said Brother. "Your ring-toss and milk-bottle games are crooked!"

"Yeah!" said Queenie. "Absolutely, totally *crooked!*"

"Nobody can win anything!" said Fred.

"Except dolls," said Sister. She was holding hers.

"Exactly, my little gumdrop," said Ralph, patting Sister's head as the cubs filed out of the booth. "All the better to make big bucks for Dr. Gert's new hospital wing."

"The only game that *isn't* crooked is the Walking Charlie," said Brother.

"Don't count on it," Ralph chuckled. He led them inside the Walking Charlie booth. "To win a valuable prize," he said, "you have to knock this 'tin can' over. But do you see this little piece of rubber hose attached to it? That makes it bounce right back up when it's hit." He patted the "tin can." "Yes, sir," he said proudly. "Crookeder than a dog's hind leg!"

"They're *all* crooked!" said Brother. "We could tell Chief Bruno!"

"And the newspaper!" said Queenie.

"Yes, you could," said Ralph calmly. "And the chief would shut the circus down right away, and Dr. Gert wouldn't get her wonderful new hospital wing. And that, my little friends, would break the poor lady's heart! Is that what you want to do? *Break Dr. Gert's heart?*"

The cubs were silent.

"You've got me all wrong," said Ralph with a little whimper. "My crooked games

are making a lot of money for a good cause. Besides, nobody's really getting hurt. Everyone's having a great time. Now, off with you! But be back here around opening time tonight. I'm gonna need your help with the games."

The cubs headed for the main tent to see if anyone there needed help. As they walked, they thought hard about what Ralph had said.

"He's right," Queenie said after a while. "We'd better not squeal on him."

"I agree," said Brother. "Besides, I have a feeling there's something even crookeder around here than Ralph's midway games."

"Like what?" asked Sister.

"I don't know," said Brother. "The whole circus, maybe. Captain Billy is an old friend of Ralph's, isn't he? I don't trust him. We might need to do some more investigating. And we won't be able to if the circus gets shut down now because of Ralph's games."

"And we wouldn't get to go in the Freaky Funhouse, either," said Queenie.

The cubs said nothing for a time.

"Tonight," said Brother at last. "We'll do it first thing tonight before helping Ralph on the midway. Agreed?"

The others looked at each other to see who would chicken out. But no one did.

"Agreed," said Cousin Fred. "First thing tonight."

Chapter 8
Funhouse Freak-out

The cubs didn't do any more investigating that afternoon. In fact, they didn't even think about it. All they thought about was the Freaky Funhouse. And the more they thought about it, the more nervous they got.

A few minutes before opening time, the cubs stood in front of the funhouse. They stared once again at the huge spooky painting.

Queenie gulped. "Well, what are we waiting for?" she said. "Let's get it over with."

"We're waiting for them to turn it on, dummy," said Cousin Fred.

WARNING:
ONLY BEARS WITH
STRONG HEARTS
MAY ENTER.

EXIT

ENTRANCE

"Oh, right," said Queenie. "I forgot."

Exactly at opening time, the Freaky Fun-house sprang into action. The neon lights blinked on. Machines creaked and groaned inside. Shrieks and moans filled the twilight.

"Maybe we'd better go straight to the midway," said Sister. "Ralph said to be there at opening time."

"He said *around* opening time, Sis," Brother reminded her. "Come on. Nobody chickens out this time."

The cubs showed their passes to the operator and stepped through a curtain. It was pitch-black inside.

"This is too scary," whispered Sister. "I can't see my hand in front of my face…"

At that instant, a bright light flashed on for a split second and a loud alarm went off. The cubs yelled and jumped straight up in the air.

"Whoa!" cried Queenie. "What was that?!"

"I don't know," said Sister. "All I saw was my hand."

A creepy voice started laughing—"hoo hoo ha ha Ha HA HAAAA!!!" A creaky door swung open to reveal a dimly lit room. The cubs clung to each other. Hearts pounding,

they inched forward into the murky gloom.

First they felt cobwebs brush against their faces. Then giant black spiders dangled before them. Finally, bursts of air shot up from holes in the floor. The cubs screamed again and again.

"Let's get out of here!" wailed Sister. "Where's the exit?!"

"Over there!" said Fred. He pointed to the red exit sign at the back of the room.

The cubs headed for the sign. But they

THE FRANKENBEAR MONSTER!

stopped dead in their tracks when a light suddenly came on and lit up the terrifying face of...

"THE FRANKENBEAR MONSTER!" cried the cubs all at once.

Behind the Monster stood a group of twisting, howling ghosts and goblins. Screeching mechanical bats flew in circles over the cubs' heads. The cubs turned white with terror!

Suddenly, without warning, the Monster's ugly mouth moved. *"Yes, mas-ter-r-r-r..."* His huge hands reached toward them!

To get to the exit, the cubs would have to run right *under* the Monster's outstretched arms!

Maybe it was courage. Maybe it was just plain fear. But whatever it was, the cubs moved. They dashed past the swaying Frankenbear Monster and tumbled through the exit curtain.

Safely outside, the cubs picked themselves up off the ground. They were breathing really hard. Their hearts pounded like jackhammers.

"I'm not going back in *there!*" gasped Cousin Fred. "At least, not *this* year!"

"I'm not going back in there...*ever!*" cried Sister.

Shaky but proud, the cubs headed for the midway.

They worked hard all evening helping Ralph run his games. Brother found it so exciting being part of the circus that he forgot all about his suspicions.

But late in the evening, near closing time, something happened that made Brother's suspicions come rushing back.

When Too-Tall threw his first baseball at a stack of wooden milk bottles, he hit the bottom three as hard as anyone ever could. But only the top bottles fell.

"Hey, this game's a cheat!" he cried. "There's something funny about those bottles!"

Brother, who was running the game, suddenly remembered the secret words Ralph had told him to use in case of trouble. "Hey, Rube!" he yelled at the top of his lungs.

It worked. Right away two big, tough circus hands came running. They grabbed

Too-Tall and his gang by their collars and walked them off the circus grounds.

That does it, thought Brother. Those guys work for Captain Billy, not Ralph. That proves Captain Billy is in on Ralph's crooked games. And if Captain Billy is crooked, then the whole circus is probably crooked!

And that's when it hit Brother.

He realized that if a crooked circus could swindle the public...*it could swindle Dr. Gert, too!*

Chapter 9
A Change of Heart

The next day, Brother called a meeting at the Burger Bear. The four cubs sat in their favorite booth and talked about Brother's suspicions.

"I really don't think we should worry," said Cousin Fred. "Like I said before, Dr. Gert's a smart cookie."

In spite of the frown on his face, Brother nodded. "I know she is," he said. "And last night, Mama and Papa told us that the hospital will get eighty percent of the money from the circus. They said Dr. Gert read the contract carefully before signing it. She even has a copy of it." He paused. "But there's still something fishy about this whole thing. We need to investigate. Problem is, I don't know where to start…"

Deep in thought, Brother gazed out the window. "Hey, look," he said. "There's Dr. Gert now."

Across the street, Dr. Gert had come out of the hospital with a group that included Mama and Papa Bear. She was showing the building-fund committee where the new wing would be built. The outline of the new wing was staked out on the grass with string. At Dr. Gert's side was Ralph Ripoff.

There Ralph stood on the hospital lawn with some of the most respected citizens of Beartown. As he listened to Dr. Gert

71

describe the new wing, with its clinic and cubs' ward, he began to feel almost like a solid citizen himself. Ralph may have been a swindler, but he liked the bears he swindled. He wanted them to have the best hospital they could.

Suddenly Ralph remembered what he had told the cubs on the midway—that if Dr. Gert didn't get her new hospital wing, *it would break her heart*. Ralph couldn't help liking Dr. Gert. He certainly didn't want to see her heart get broken.

Then Ralph turned his thoughts to his old friend Captain Billy. Billy had told him that he would take only sixty percent of the circus money and pay all the expenses with it. That would leave a lot of money for the hospital. But now Ralph wondered if Billy had lied to *him*. He knew from experience that there were all kinds of swindlers. And some of them just couldn't be trusted!

Ralph decided to have a look at the contract that Billy had tricked Dr. Gert into signing. He couldn't ask to see Dr. Gert's or Mayor Honeypot's copies. That would make them suspicious. He knew he'd have to check the one that must be in Captain Billy's office—the one Billy had pretended was for the "main" office. Ralph knew that Billy's office *was* the main office.

Ralph quickly said good-bye to Dr. Gert and the others. Walking fast, he headed down the street toward the highway.

Brother spotted him from the window of the Burger Bear. "Ralph's up to something," he said. "Let's follow him!"

Chapter 10
Spying for Dollars

The cubs followed Ralph to the circus grounds. It was hours before opening time, and only a few workers were on the job. Ralph went straight to the lead truck, looked around to see if anyone was watching, and climbed into Captain Billy's office.

From their hiding place behind another truck, the cubs could see Captain Billy and Otto heading for the office.

"Come on," said Brother. "We can listen from inside the funhouse."

"Are you kidding?" said Sister. "I'm not going back in *there!*"

"It isn't even turned on," said Brother. "Besides, we *have* to. They're probably planning how to swindle Dr. Gert!"

The cubs raced to the funhouse and slipped inside. Shivering with fear, they pushed their way through cobwebs—past silent ghosts and goblins, and under the motionless arms of the Frankenbear Monster—until they reached the front wall next to the office. They could hear angry voices coming from inside.

High in the wall was an air vent. The cubs climbed on each other's shoulders so that Sister could peer through it.

"Goin' through our files, eh?" Captain Billy was saying. "Caught you red-handed."

"Show me a copy of that contract you tricked Gert into signing!" cried Ralph.

"*I* tricked Gert into signing?" said Billy. "What about *you?* What's gotten into you, Ralph? Gone soft on the old doctor?"

"Don't be ridiculous," said Ralph. "But this is *my* town, and these are *my* suckers. And I'm not gonna let you and your big ape here—"

"One more word outta you, and I'll crush you like a grape!" growled Otto.

Ralph stumbled toward the door. "I'd like to see you try, you big creep!" he muttered. But he left quickly, slamming the door behind him.

"Should I go after him, boss?" asked Otto.

"Don't bother," said Billy. "We're closing down and moving out after tonight's fireworks, anyway."

"What about the doctor?"

"No problem," said Billy. "I'll deliver her share of the take myself. Twenty percent minus all our expenses. And it's all legal, according to the contracts Dr. Gert signed after reading that first phony one!"

Billy and Otto laughed as they left the office.

Just then Brother got a cramp in his leg and fell sideways. The tower of cubs came tumbling down. There they lay in a heap of

rubber cobwebs, spiders, and bats. They stayed put until they were sure Billy and Otto wouldn't notice them leaving. Then they quickly scrambled through the exit and headed back to town.

"Did you hear that?" said Queenie when they reached the highway. "Twenty percent minus expenses! That'll leave hardly anything for the hospital!"

"You bet I heard it," said Brother. "And if we can't get our hands on some real evidence of this swindle, Captain Billy will walk off with almost all the money."

"What kind of evidence?" asked Sister.

"The first contract Dr. Gert signed," said Brother. "We've got to find it."

Chapter 11
Running Away with the Circus?

At the circus that evening, the crowds were enormous. As the cubs worked on the midway, they took turns slipping away to keep watch on Captain Billy's office. They were waiting for him to leave so they could sneak in and find the contract that would prove Dr. Gert had been swindled. With that contract in hand, they figured, Chief Bruno could arrest Captain Billy and give the stolen money to the hospital.

Toward the end of the evening, Queenie came running to the ring-toss game, where

Brother was working. "Captain Billy just left the office," she said. "He even left the circus grounds."

"Now's our chance," said Brother. "Go tell Sister and Fred." He turned to the line of customers. "Sorry, folks. The ring toss is closing up. Why not try Ralph's Walking Charlie game over there?"

The cubs met up at the office door.

"Look!" said Cousin Fred, pointing to the sky. "The fireworks are starting!"

"Those fireworks are nothing compared to the ones that'll go off if we get caught in this office!" said Brother.

The cubs slipped into the office and began looking through the file cabinets and desk drawers.

Meanwhile, Captain Billy was already ringing Dr. Gert Grizzly's doorbell. When she answered it, he handed her an envelope. "Here's your share of the take, Doctor," he said. "You'd better count it."

Dr. Gert emptied the envelope into her hand. She stared at the tiny pile of money. "Fourteen dollars and seventeen cents?" she said. *"Fourteen dollars and seventeen cents?!* I don't understand! My contract says..." She hurried inside and came back reading her copy of the contract. " '...*twenty percent...minus all expenses...*' Oh, dear. Oh, *dear!* I've been tricked!"

Captain Billy unrolled a long sheet of

paper. "Here's the list of expenses, Gert. Look it over when you have a minute." He dropped the list at her feet. "Well, ta-ta. It's been nice knowing you, Doctor. Profitable, too."

Only moments after Billy had left, Ralph Ripoff came running to Dr. Gert's door. She was on her knees, staring down at the list of expenses. And she was crying.

FOURTEEN DOLLARS AND SEVENTEEN CENTS?!!

"He's gone already," gasped Ralph. "I couldn't keep up with him." He helped the doctor to her feet and took the contract from her hand. "Let me see that... *Twenty percent! Minus all expenses...!* Is this all the money he paid you?"

Ralph counted it. The bellow he let out was heard all over the neighborhood.

"FOURTEEN DOLLARS AND SEVENTEEN CENTS?!! Why, that no-good, low-down...*swindler!* Don't worry, my dear! I won't let him get away with this!"

Ralph dashed off toward the circus grounds.

Meanwhile, in Captain Billy's office, the cubs were still searching for the contract.

"We need that original contract," said Brother. "Without it we can't prove that Captain Billy's a fraud. Keep looking. It has to be here..."

"If it proves he's a fraud, he probably hid it really well," said Cousin Fred. "Find anything, Queenie?"

"Nope," said Queenie. "What about you, Sis?"

Sister had one hand in the wastebasket beside Captain Billy's desk. "Just a bunch of crumpled notes," she said. "And some torn bits of paper…"

As her hand touched the torn bits of paper, Sister got a funny feeling. Maybe Captain Billy had hidden the contract. *And maybe he hadn't…*

Just then Brother looked out the window. "Oh, no!" he cried. "Here come Captain Billy and Otto!"

"Quick!" said Fred. "Put a chair on the desk! We can climb through the air vent into the funhouse!"

The cubs scrambled through the air vent

as fast as they could. Brother was last. As he slid through the vent, he gave the chair a kick that knocked it off the desk and onto the floor. And just in the nick of time!

Captain Billy and Otto climbed into the office. Otto picked up the chair lying on the floor. "Hey, boss," he said. "Looks like Ralph was here snooping around again."

"What a loser," said Billy with a laugh. "Well, we're ready to roll. Go lock up the funhouse."

Huddled against the front wall, the cubs could hear Otto at the rear of the trailer. He locked the entrance, then the exit. They were trapped in the Freaky Funhouse!

Just then the cubs heard the office door open and someone climb in. Ralph Ripoff's voice cried out, "You can't do this, Billy!"

"Oh, yeah?" sneered Otto, climbing in after Ralph. "We're doin' it, Mr. Wise Guy!"

There was a struggle, but it didn't last long. With just one punch, the World's Strongest Bear knocked Ralph to the floor.

"Tie him up," ordered Captain Billy. "And

gag him, too. I don't want to listen to him yappin' when he wakes up."

Not long afterward, Captain Billy started

the engine. The cubs felt the big truck begin to move.

"Poor Ralph," whispered Sister.

"What d'ya mean 'poor Ralph'?" Queenie whispered back. "What about poor *us!*"

"I always wondered what it would be like to run away with the circus," said Cousin Fred. "But I never dreamed the circus would run away with *me!*"

Chapter 12
Ralph Takes a Dive

As the truck rolled on, the cubs looked around at the spooky robots. In the darkness, the Frankenbear Monster was even more frightening than when it was all lit up and moving.

"I'm scared!" Sister whined.

But even scarier than the Frankenbear Monster was what the cubs heard next. Captain Billy had left on the intercom in the office, so the cubs could hear what was being said in the cab of the truck.

"Hey, boss," said Otto. "What're we gonna do about Ripoff?"

"We'll have to get rid of him," said Captain Billy. "Goin' soft on that doctor might

make him talk. It'd just be his word against ours, but I'm not takin' any chances. The bridge over Great Roaring River is a couple miles ahead. We'll dump him in the river."

"Good thinkin', boss," said Otto.

By now the cubs were so scared that they had to put their hands over one another's mouths to keep each other from screaming. Captain Billy and Otto probably couldn't

hear what was happening in the funhouse, but the cubs were taking no chances. They didn't want to join Ralph at the bottom of Great Roaring River!

Soon the truck slowed down and pulled to a stop. The cubs heard Captain Billy climb down from the cab and yell to the passing circus trucks to meet him at the next town. Then they heard Otto grunting under the weight of Ralph's plump body.

Seconds later, there was a splash far below.

Captain Billy started the truck again. "The Riverside Roadhouse is right at the end of the bridge," he told Otto. "Let's celebrate with a little snack."

"Great idea," said Otto. "There's something about getting rid of a witness that gives me an appetite."

The cubs saw their chance. As soon as Captain Billy and Otto were gone, they squeezed through the air vent and into the office and dialed 911 on the car phone.

Within minutes, Chief Bruno came roaring up with five other police cars. The cubs piled out of the office and told the chief everything they had seen and heard. Chief Bruno ordered his officers into the Riverside Roadhouse. Moments later they came back with Captain Billy and Otto in handcuffs.

"Put those birds in the back of my squad

car!" barked Chief Bruno. "And keep a good eye on 'em!" He turned to the cubs. "They'll go to jail for the rest of their lives for the murder of Ralph Ripoff."

The chief took off his cap and placed it over his heart. "I'm sure Ralph would be grateful to you cubs for catching them," he said sadly.

"Poor Ralph," said Sister. She started to cry.

Queenie was more angry than sad. "What about fraud?" she said. "Captain Billy swindled Dr. Gert! I'll bet the stolen money is somewhere in that office!"

"In a hidden safe, most likely," said Chief Bruno.

"I'll bet it's behind the painting of Coco

the Clown!" said Cousin Fred. "Let's go break it open!"

"Hold on, now," said Chief Bruno. "I'm afraid we can't give any of that money to the hospital without some real solid evidence of fraud."

"Like the original contract that Dr. Gert read and signed?" asked Brother.

"Exactly," said the chief. "But I don't think we'll ever find it. Captain Billy may be a crook, but he's no fool. He must have destroyed it."

Suddenly Sister remembered something

that she had forgotten in all the excitement. Her eyes lit up. She dashed to the truck office.

"What's she up to?" said Queenie.

"Let's take a look," said Brother.

With Chief Bruno right behind them, the cubs hurried to the office. They found Sister sitting at Captain Billy's desk with a bunch of torn pieces of paper spread out in front of her.

"I noticed these earlier in the wastebasket," she said. "Hey, look! This one says *Gert* on it in handwriting! And this one says *Contract!*"

It took less than a minute for the cubs to fit the pieces of paper together like a jigsaw puzzle.

"I was right!" cried Sister. "It's the missing contract!"

"Well, I'll be darned!" said Chief Bruno.

"We're sure lucky it's still here."

"Coco the Clown doubles as the circus custodian," said Cousin Fred. "I'll bet he was so busy with the big trash cans on the circus grounds that he forgot to empty Captain Billy's wastebasket!"

"Great work, Sister!" said the chief, beaming. "I can't wait to see the look on Captain Billy's face when I tell him the news!"

CONTRACT

AGREEMENT MADE BETWEEN CAPTAIN BILLY'S CIRCUS AND DR. GERT GRIZZLY, WHEREAS, CAPTAIN BILLY WILL PAY 80% OFF ALL MONEYS COLLECTED AT SPECIAL BENEFIT CIRCUS CARNIVAL IN BEA

Chapter 13
Good-bye to Ralph Ripoff?

The look on Captain Billy's face when he found out about the contract wasn't a happy one. But neither were the looks on the faces of Beartown's citizens when they found out what had happened to Ralph Ripoff. Although Ralph had been a swindler for most of his life, many bears liked him. And they were very sad indeed that he was gone.

Until, that is, a few hours later, when Officer Marguerite found Ralph still very much alive, resting at his houseboat.

It was lucky for Ralph that he hadn't

always been a swindler. Not only had he been a pickpocket and a games operator when he was younger, he had also been an escape artist in a magic show. And that's just how he'd escaped from the chilly waters of Great Roaring River. He had managed to slip out of his ropes before running out of breath.

The charges against Captain Billy and Otto were changed from fraud and murder to fraud and attempted murder. They were put on trial, found guilty, and sent off to Bear Country Prison in Big Bear City.

As for Dr. Gert Grizzly, she got all the money she needed for the new hospital wing. Chief Bruno had found it in the safe in Captain Billy's office—which *was* behind the picture of Coco the Clown.

And when Dr. Gert heard about the rumor that she had a crush on Ralph Ripoff,

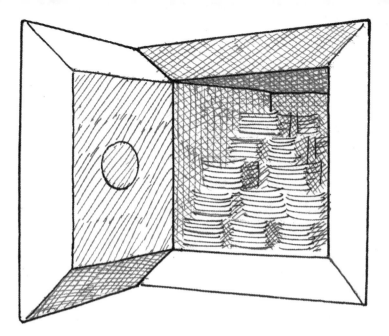

she just laughed. She had only been grateful to Ralph for his help in raising money for the hospital.

Quicker than you can say "Captain Billy's Colossal Circus and Carnival," everything returned to normal in Bear Country. Even Ralph Ripoff. Ralph never did become a solid citizen. He may have been a goodhearted swindler. But he was still a swindler at heart.

There was one thing about Ralph that did change, though. For the rest of his long, dishonest life—even in the hottest summer weather—he never *ever* went swimming in Great Roaring River again.

Stan and Jan Berenstain began writing and illustrating books for children in the early 1960s, when their two young sons were beginning to read. That marked the start of the best-selling Berenstain Bears series. Now, with more than one hundred books in print, videos, television shows, and even Berenstain Bears attractions at major amusement parks, it's hard to tell where the Bears end and the Berenstains begin!

Stan and Jan make their home in Bucks County, Pennsylvania, near their sons—Leo, a writer, and Michael, an illustrator—who are helping them with Big Chapter Books stories and pictures. They plan on writing and illustrating many more books for children, especially for their four grandchildren, who keep them well in touch with the kids of today.